father's unemployment and another relative's bankruptcy, both of them   by the fledgling writer. To make matter   ylor Coleridge publicly deno   and loathsome, and "me   the depravation of the public mind," going   so far as to decry it as atheistic. The Church of Ireland took note of these and earlier criticisms and, having discovered the identity of Bertram's author (Maturin had shed his nom de plume to collect the profits from the play), subsequently barred Maturin's further clerical advancement. Forced to support his wife and four children by writing (his salary as curate was £80-90 per annum, compared to the £1000 he made for Bertram), he switched back from playwright to novelist after a string of his plays met with failure. Maturin died in Dublin on 30 October 1824, after which rumours (none of them confirmed or proven) circulated that he had committed suicide. Honoré de Balzac and Charles Baudelaire later expressed fondness for Maturin's work, particularly his most famous novel, Melmoth the Wanderer.

Introduction

Balzac likens the hero of one of his short stories to "Moliere's Don Juan, Goethe's Faust, Byron's Manfred, Maturin's Melmoth—great allegorical figures drawn by the greatest men of genius in Europe."

"But what is 'Melmoth'? Why is HE classed as 'a great allegorical figure'?" exclaimed many a surprised reader. Few had perused—few know at this day—the terrible story of Melmoth the Wanderer, half man, half devil, who has bartered away his soul for the glory of power and knowledge, and, repenting of his bargain, tries again and again to persuade some desperate human to change places with him— penetrates to the refuge of misery, the death chamber, even the madhouse, seeking one in such utter agony as to accept his help, and take his curse—but ever fails.

Why this extraordinary tale, told with wild and compelling sweep, has remained so deep in oblivion, appears immediately on a glance at the original. The author, Charles Robert Maturin, a

Melmoth the Wanderer (Lock and Key Version)

Charles Robert Maturin

About Maturin:

Charles Robert Maturin, also known as C.R. Maturin (born September 25, 1782 in Dublin; died October 30, 1824 in Dublin) was an Anglo-Irish Protestant clergyman (ordained by the Church of Ireland) and a writer of gothic plays and novels. Descended from a Huguenot family, he attended Trinity College, Dublin. Shortly after being ordained as curate of Loughrea in 1803, he married acclaimed singer Henrietta Kingsbury, a sister of Sarah Kingsbury, whose daughter, Jane Wilde, was the mother of Oscar Wilde. Thus Charles Maturin was Oscar Wilde's great-uncle by marriage. His first three works were published under the pseudonym Dennis Jasper Murphy and were critical and commercial failures. They did, however, catch the attention of Sir Walter Scott, who recommended Maturin's work to Lord Byron. With the help of these two literary luminaries, the curate's play, Bertram (staged at Drury Lane for 22 nights) saw a wider audience and became a success. Financial success, however, eluded Maturin, as the play's run coincided with his needy, eccentric Irish clergyman of 1780–1824, could cause intense suspense and horror—could read keenly into human motives—could teach an awful moral lesson in the guise of fascinating fiction, but he could not stick to a long story with simplicity. His dozens of shifting scenes, his fantastic coils of "tales within tales" sadly perplex the reader of "Melmoth" in the first version. It is hoped, however, that the present selection, by its directness and the clearness of the story thread, may please the modern reader better than the involved original, and bring before a wider public some of the most gripping descriptions ever penned in English.

In Volume IV of these stories comes a tale, "Melmoth Reconciled," which Balzac himself wrote, while under the spell of Maturin's "great allegorical figure." Here the unhappy being succeeds in his purpose. The story takes place in mocking, careless Paris, "that branch establishment of hell"; a cashier, on the eve of embezzlement and detection, cynically accedes to Melmoth's terms, and accepts his help—with what unlooked-for results, the reader may see.

Melmoth the Wanderer

John Melmoth, student at Trinity College, Dublin, having journeyed to County Wicklow for attendance at the deathbed of his miserly uncle, finds the old man, even in his last moments, tortured by avarice, and by suspicion of all around him. He whispers to John:

"I want a glass of wine, it would keep me alive for some hours, but there is not one I can trust to get it for me,—they'd steal a bottle, and ruin me." John was greatly shocked. "Sir, for God's sake, let ME get a glass of wine for you." "Do you know where?" said the old man, with an expression in his face John could not understand. "No, Sir; you know I have been rather a stranger here, Sir." "Take this key," said old Melmoth, after a violent spasm; "take this key, there is wine in that closet,— Madeira. I always told them there was nothing there, but they did not believe me, or I should not have been robbed as I have been. At one time I said it was whisky, and then I fared worse than ever, for they drank twice as much of it."

John took the key from his uncle's hand; the dying man pressed it as he did so, and John, interpreting this as a mark of kindness, returned the pressure.

He was undeceived by the whisper that followed, —"John, my lad, don't drink any of that wine while you are there." "Good God!" said John, indignantly throwing the key on the bed; then, recollecting that the miserable being before him was no object of resentment, he gave the promise required, and entered the closet, which no foot but that of old Melmoth had entered for nearly sixty years. He had some difficulty in finding out the wine, and indeed stayed long enough to justify his uncle's suspicions,—but his mind was agitated, and his hand unsteady. He could not but remark his uncle's extraordinary look, that had the ghastliness of fear superadded to that of death, as he gave him permission to enter his closet. He could not but see the looks of horror which the women exchanged as he approached it. And, finally, when he was in it, his memory was malicious enough to suggest some faint traces of a story, too horrible for imagination, connected with it. He remembered in one moment most distinctly, that no one but his uncle had ever been known to enter it for many years.

Before he quitted it, he held up the dim light, and looked around him with a mixture of terror and curiosity. There was a great deal of decayed and useless lumber, such as might be supposed to be heaped up to rot in a miser's closet; but John's eyes were in a moment, and as if by magic, riveted on a portrait that hung on the wall, and appeared, even to his untaught eye, far superior to the tribe of family pictures that are left to molder on the walls of a family mansion. It represented a man of middle age. There was nothing remarkable in the costume,

or in the countenance, but THE EYES, John felt, were such as one feels they wish they had never seen, and feels they can never forget. Had he been acquainted with the poetry of Southey, he might have often exclaimed in his after-life,
"Only the eyes had life,
They gleamed with demon light."—THALABA.
From an impulse equally resistless and painful, he approached the portrait, held the candle toward it, and could distinguish the words on the border of the painting,—Jno. Melmoth, anno 1646. John was neither timid by nature, nor nervous by constitution, nor superstitious from habit, yet he continued to gaze in stupid horror on this singular picture, till, aroused by his uncle's cough, he hurried into his room. The old man swallowed the wine. He appeared a little revived; it was long since he had tasted such a cordial,—his heart appeared to expand to a momentary confidence. "John, what did you see in that room?" "Nothing, Sir." "That's a lie; everyone wants to cheat or to rob me." "Sir, I don't want to do either." "Well, what did you see that you—you took notice of?" "Only a picture,

Sir." "A picture, Sir!—the original is still alive." John, though under the impression of his recent feelings, could not but look incredulous. "John," whispered his uncle;— "John, they say I am dying of this and that; and one says it is for want of nourishment, and one says it is for want of medicine,—but, John," and his face looked hideously ghastly, "I am dying of a fright. That man," and he extended his meager arm toward the closet, as if he was pointing to a living being; "that man, I have good reason to know, is alive still." "How is that possible, Sir?" said John involuntarily, "the date on the picture is 1646." "You have seen it, —you have noticed it," said his uncle. "Well,"—he rocked and nodded on his bolster for a moment, then, grasping John's hand with an unutterable look, he exclaimed, "You will see him again, he is alive." Then, sinking back on his bolster, he fell into a kind of sleep or stupor, his eyes still open, and fixed on John.

The house was now perfectly silent, and John had time and space for reflection. More thoughts came crowding on him than he wished to welcome, but they would not be repulsed. He thought of his uncle's habits and character, turned the matter over and over again in his mind, and he said to himself, "The last man on earth to be superstitious. He never thought of anything but the price of stocks, and the rate of exchange, and my college expenses, that hung heavier at his heart than all; and such a man to die of a fright,—a ridiculous fright, that a man living 150 years ago is alive still, and yet—he is dying." John paused, for facts will confute the most stubborn logician. "With all his hardness of mind, and of heart, he is dying of a fright. I heard it in the kitchen, I have heard it from himself,—he could not be deceived. If I had ever heard he was nervous, or fanciful, or superstitious, but a character so contrary to all these impressions;—a man that, as poor Butler says, in his 'Remains of the Antiquarian,' would have 'sold Christ over again for the numerical piece of silver which Judas got for him,'—such a man to die of fear! Yet he IS dying," said John, glancing his fearful eye on the contracted nostril, the glazed eye, the drooping jaw, the whole horrible apparatus of the facies

Hippocraticae displayed, and soon to cease its display.

Old Melmoth at this moment seemed to be in a deep stupor; his eyes lost that little expression they had before, and his hands, that had convulsively been catching at the blankets, let go their short and quivering grasp, and lay extended on the bed like the claws of some bird that had died of hunger,—so meager, so yellow, so spread. John, unaccustomed to the sight of death, believed this to be only a sign that he was going to sleep; and, urged by an impulse for which he did not attempt to account to himself, caught up the miserable light, and once more ventured into the forbidden room,— the BLUE CHAMBER of the dwelling. The motion roused the dying man;—he sat bolt upright in his bed. This John could not see, for he was now in the closet; but he heard the groan, or rather the choked and gurgling rattle of the throat, that announces the horrible conflict between muscular and mental convulsion. He started, turned away; but, as he turned away, he thought he saw the eyes of the portrait, on which his own was fixed, MOVE, and hurried back to his uncle's bedside.

Old Melmoth died in the course of that night, and died as he had lived, in a kind of avaricious delirium. John could not have imagined a scene so horrible as his last hours presented. He cursed and blasphemed about three halfpence, missing, as he said, some weeks before, in an account of change with his groom, about hay to a starved horse that he kept. Then he grasped John's hand, and asked him to give him the sacrament. "If I send to the clergyman, he will charge me something for it, which I cannot pay,— I cannot. They say I am rich, —look at this blanket;—but I would not mind that, if I could save my soul." And, raving, he added, "Indeed, Doctor, I am a very poor man. I never troubled a clergyman before, and all I want is, that you will grant me two trifling requests, very little matters in your way,—save my soul, and (whispering) make interest to get me a parish coffin,—I have not enough left to bury me. I always told everyone I was poor, but the more I told them so, the less they believed me."

John, greatly shocked, retired from the bedside, and

sat down in a distant corner of the room. The women were again in the room, which was very dark. Melmoth was silent from exhaustion, and there was a deathlike pause for some time. At this moment John saw the door open, and a figure appear at it, who looked round the room, and then quietly and deliberately retired, but not before John had discovered in his face the living original of the portrait. His first impulse was to utter an exclamation of terror, but his breath felt stopped. He was then rising to pursue the figure, but a moment's reflection checked him. What could be more absurd, than to be alarmed or amazed at a resemblance between a living man and the portrait of a dead one! The likeness was doubtless strong enough to strike him even in that darkened room, but it was doubtless only a likeness; and though it might be imposing enough to terrify an old man of gloomy and retired habits, and with a broken constitution, John resolved it should not produce the same effect on him.

But while he was applauding himself for this resolution, the door opened, and the figure appeared at it, beckoning and nodding to him, with a familiarity somewhat terrifying. John now started up, determined to pursue it; but the pursuit was stopped by the weak but shrill cries of his uncle, who was struggling at once with the agonies of death and his housekeeper. The poor woman, anxious for her master's reputation and her own, was trying to put on him a clean shirt and nightcap, and Melmoth, who had just sensation enough to perceive they were taking something from him, continued exclaiming feebly, "They are robbing me,—robbing me in my last moments,—robbing a dying man. John, won't you assist me,—I shall die a beggar; they are taking my last shirt,—I shall die a beggar."—And the miser died.

.. . ..

A few days after the funeral, the will was opened before proper witnesses, and John was found to be left sole heir to his uncle's property, which, though originally moderate, had, by his grasping habits, and parsimonious life, become very considerable.

As the attorney who read the will concluded, he added, "There are some words here, at the corner of the parchment, which do not appear to be part of the will, as they are neither in the form of a codicil, nor is the signature of the testator affixed to them; but, to the best of my belief, they are in the handwriting of the deceased." As he spoke he showed the lines to Melmoth, who immediately recognized his uncle's hand (that perpendicular and penurious hand, that seems determined to make the most of the very paper, thriftily abridging every word, and leaving scarce an atom of margin), and read, not without some emotion, the following words: "I enjoin my nephew and heir, John Melmoth, to remove, destroy, or cause to be destroyed, the portrait inscribed J. Melmoth, 1646, hanging in my closet. I also enjoin him to search for a manuscript, which I think he will find in the third and lowest left-hand drawer of the mahogany chest standing under that portrait,—it is among some papers of no value, such as manuscript sermons, and pamphlets on the improvement of Ireland, and such stuff; he will distinguish it by its being tied round with a black tape, and the paper being very moldy and discolored. He may read it if he will;—I think he had better not. At all events, I adjure him, if there be any power in the adjuration of a dying man, to burn it."

After reading this singular memorandum, the business of the meeting was again resumed; and as old Melmoth's will was very clear and legally worded, all was soon settled, the party dispersed, and John Melmoth was left alone.

. . . . .

He resolutely entered the closet, shut the door, and proceeded to search for the manuscript. It was soon found, for the directions of old Melmoth were forcibly written, and strongly remembered. The manuscript, old, tattered, and discolored, was taken from the very drawer in which it was mentioned to be laid. Melmoth's hands felt as cold as those of his dead uncle, when he drew the blotted pages from their nook. He sat down to read,—there was a dead silence through the house. Melmoth looked wistfully at the candles, snuffed them, and still thought they looked dim, (perchance he thought they burned blue, but such thought he kept to himself). Certain it is, he often changed his posture, and would have changed his chair, had there been more than one in the apartment.

He sank for a few moments into a fit of gloomy abstraction, till the sound of the clock striking twelve made him start,—it was the only sound he had heard for some hours, and the sounds produced by inanimate things, while all living beings around are as dead, have at such an hour an effect indescribably awful. John looked at his manuscript with some reluctance, opened it, paused over the first lines, and as the wind sighed round the desolate apartment, and the rain pattered with a mournful sound against the dismantled window, wished—what did he wish for?—he wished the sound of the wind less dismal, and the dash of the rain less monotonous.—He may be forgiven, it was past midnight, and there was not a human being awake but himself within ten miles when he began to read.

. . . . .

The manuscript was discolored, obliterated, and mutilated beyond any that had ever before exercised the patience of a reader. Michaelis himself, scrutinizing into the pretended autograph of St. Mark at Venice, never had a harder time of it. —Melmoth could make out only a sentence here and there. The writer, it appeared, was an Englishman of the name of Stanton, who had traveled abroad shortly after the Restoration.

Traveling was not then attended with the facilities which modern improvement has introduced, and scholars and literati, the intelligent, the idle, and the curious, wandered over the Continent for years, like Tom Corvat, though they had the modesty, on their return, to entitle the result of their multiplied observations and labors only "crudities."

Stanton, about the year 1676, was in Spain; he was, like most of the travelers of that age, a man of literature, intelligence, and curiosity, but ignorant of the language of the country, and fighting his way at times from convent to convent, in quest of what was called "Hospitality," that is, obtaining board and lodging on the condition of holding a debate in Latin, on some point theological or metaphysical, with any monk who would become the champion of the strife. Now, as the theology was Catholic, and the metaphysics Aristotelian, Stanton sometimes wished himself at the miserable Posada from whose filth and famine he had been fighting his escape; but though his reverend antagonists always denounced his creed, and comforted themselves, even in defeat, with the assurance that he must be damned, on the double score of his being a heretic and an Englishman, they were obliged to confess that his Latin was good, and his logic unanswerable; and he was allowed, in most cases, to sup and sleep in peace. This was not doomed to be his fate on the night of the 17th August 1677, when he found himself in the plains of Valencia, deserted by a cowardly guide, who had been terrified by the sight of a cross erected as a memorial of a murder, had slipped off his mule unperceived, crossing himself every step he took on his retreat from the heretic, and left Stanton amid the terrors of an approaching storm, and the dangers of an unknown country. The sublime and yet softened beauty of the scenery around, had filled the soul of Stanton with delight, and he enjoyed that delight as Englishmen generally do, silently.

The magnificent remains of two dynasties that had passed away, the ruins of Roman palaces, and of Moorish fortresses, were around and above him;— the dark and heavy thunder clouds that advanced slowly, seemed like the shrouds of these specters of departed greatness; they approached, but did not yet overwhelm or conceal them, as if Nature herself was for once awed by the power of man; and far below, the lovely valley of Valencia blushed and burned in all the glory of sunset, like a bride receiving the last glowing kiss of the bridegroom before the approach of night. Stanton gazed around. The difference between the architecture of the Roman and Moorish ruins struck him. Among the former are the remains of a theater, and something like a public place; the latter present only the remains of fortresses, embattled, castellated, and fortified from top to bottom,—not a loophole for pleasure to get in by,—the loopholes were only for arrows; all denoted military power and despotic subjugation a l'outrance. The contrast might have pleased a philosopher, and he might have indulged in the reflection, that though the ancient Greeks and Romans were savages (as Dr. Johnson says all people who want a press must be, and he says truly), yet they were wonderful savages for their time, for they alone have left traces of their taste for pleasure in the countries they conquered, in their superb theaters, temples (which were also dedicated to pleasure one way or another), and baths, while other conquering bands of savages never left anything behind them but traces of their rage for power. So thought Stanton, as he still saw strongly defined, though darkened by the darkening clouds, the huge skeleton of a Roman amphitheater, its arched and gigantic colonnades now admitting a gleam of light, and now commingling with the purple thunder cloud; and now the solid and heavy mass of a Moorish fortress, no light playing between its impermeable walls,— the image of power, dark, isolated, impenetrable. Stanton forgot his cowardly guide, his loneliness, his danger amid an approaching storm and an inhospitable country, where his name and country would shut every door against him, and every peal of thunder would be supposed justified by the daring intrusion of a heretic in the dwelling of an old Christian, as the Spanish Catholics absurdly term themselves, to mark the distinction between them and the baptized Moors.

All this was forgot in contemplating the glorious

and awful scenery before him,—light struggling with darkness,—and darkness menacing a light still more terrible, and announcing its menace in the blue and livid mass of cloud that hovered like a destroying angel in the air, its arrows aimed, but their direction awfully indefinite. But he ceased to forget these local and petty dangers, as the sublimity of romance would term them, when he saw the first flash of the lightning, broad and red as the banners of an insulting army whose motto is Vae victis, shatter to atoms the remains of a Roman tower;—the rifted stones rolled down the hill, and fell at the feet of Stanton. He stood appalled, and, awaiting his summons from the Power in whose eye pyramids, palaces, and the worms whose toil has formed them, and the worms who toil out their existence under their shadow or their pressure, are perhaps all alike contemptible, he stood collected, and for a moment felt that defiance of danger which danger itself excites, and we love to encounter it as a physical enemy, to bid it "do its worst," and feel that its worst will perhaps be ultimately its best for us. He stood and saw another flash dart its bright, brief, and malignant glance over the ruins of ancient power, and the luxuriance of recent fertility. Singular contrast! The relics of art forever decaying,—the productions of nature forever renewed.—(Alas! for what purpose are they renewed, better than to mock at the perishable monuments which men try in vain to rival them by.) The pyramids themselves must perish, but the grass that grows between their disjointed stones will be renewed from year to year.

Stanton was thinking thus, when all power of

thought was suspended, by seeing two persons bearing between them the body of a young, and apparently very lovely girl, who had been struck dead by the lightning. Stanton approached, and heard the voices of the bearers repeating, "There is none who will mourn for her!" "There is none who will mourn for her!" said other voices, as two more bore in their arms the blasted and blackened figure of what had once been a man, comely and graceful; —"there is not ONE to mourn for her now!" They were lovers, and he had been consumed by the flash that had destroyed her, while in the act of endeavoring to defend her. As they were about to remove the bodies, a person approached with a calmness of step and demeanor, as if he were alone unconscious of danger, and incapable of fear; and after looking on them for some time, burst into a laugh so loud, wild, and protracted, that the peasants, starting with as much horror at the sound as at that of the storm, hurried away, bearing the corpses with them. Even Stanton's fears were subdued by his astonishment, and, turning to the stranger, who remained standing on the same spot, he asked the reason of such an outrage on humanity. The stranger, slowly turning round, and disclosing a countenance which—(Here the manuscript was illegible for a few lines), said in English—(A long hiatus followed here, and the next passage that was legible, though it proved to be a continuation of the narrative, was but a fragment.)

. . . . .

The terrors of the night rendered Stanton a sturdy and unappeasable applicant; and the shrill voice of the old woman, repeating, "no heretic—no English —Mother of God protect us—avaunt Satan!"— combined with the clatter of the wooden casement (peculiar to the houses in Valencia) which she opened to discharge her volley of anathematization, and shut again as the lightning glanced through the aperture, were unable to repel his importunate request for admittance, in a night whose terrors ought to soften all the miserable petty local passions into one awful feeling of fear for the Power who caused it, and compassion for those who were exposed to it.—But Stanton felt there was something more than national bigotry in the exclamations of the old woman; there was a peculiar and personal horror of the English.—And he was right; but this did not diminish the eagerness of his... .

... . .

The house was handsome and spacious, but the melancholy appearance of desertion ... .

... . .

—The benches were by the wall, but there were none to sit there; the tables were spread in what had been the hall, but it seemed as if none had gathered round them for many years;—the clock struck audibly, there was no voice of mirth or of occupation to drown its sound; time told his awful lesson to silence alone;—the hearths were black with fuel long since consumed;—the family portraits looked as if they were the only tenants of the mansion; they seemed to say, from their moldering frames, "there are none to gaze on us;" and the echo of the steps of Stanton and his feeble guide, was the only sound audible between the peals of thunder that rolled still awfully, but more distantly,—every peal like the exhausted murmurs of a spent heart. As they passed on, a shriek was heard. Stanton paused, and fearful images of the dangers to which travelers on the Continent are exposed in deserted and remote habitations, came into his mind. "Don't heed it," said the old woman, lighting him on with a miserable lamp;—"it is only he… .

… . .

The old woman having now satisfied herself, by ocular demonstration, that her English guest, even if he was the devil, had neither horn, hoof, nor tail, that he could bear the sign of the cross without changing his form, and that, when he spoke, not a puff of sulphur came out of his mouth, began to take courage, and at length commenced her story, which, weary and comfortless as Stanton was, … .

… . .

Every obstacle was now removed; parents and relations at last gave up all opposition, and the young pair were united. Never was there a lovelier, —they seemed like angels who had only anticipated by a few years their celestial and eternal union. The marriage was solemnized with much pomp, and a few days after there was a feast in that very wainscoted chamber which you paused to remark was so gloomy. It was that night hung with rich tapestry, representing the exploits of the Cid, particularly that of his burning a few Moors who refused to renounce their accursed religion. They were represented beautifully tortured, writhing and howling, and "Mahomet! Mahomet!" issuing out of their mouths, as they called on him in their burning agonies;—you could almost hear them scream. At the upper end of the room, under a splendid estrade, over which was an image of the blessed Virgin, sat Donna Isabella de Cardoza, mother to the bride, and near her Donna Ines, the bride, on rich almohadas; the bridegroom sat opposite to her, and though they never spoke to each other, their eyes, slowly raised, but suddenly withdrawn (those eyes that blushed), told to each other the delicious secret of their happiness. Don Pedro de Cardoza had assembled a large party in honor of his daughter's nuptials; among them was an Englishman of the name of MELMOTH, a traveler;

no one knew who had brought him there. He sat silent like the rest, while the iced waters and the sugared wafers were presented to the company. The night was intensely hot, and the moon glowed like a sun over the ruins of Saguntum; the embroidered blinds flapped heavily, as if the wind made an effort to raise them in vain, and then desisted.

(Another defect in the manuscript occurred here, but it was soon supplied.)

..... .

The company were dispersed through various alleys of the garden; the bridegroom and bride wandered through one where the delicious perfume of the orange trees mingled itself with that of the myrtles in blow. On their return to the ball, both of them asked, Had the company heard the exquisite sounds that floated through the garden just before they quitted it? No one had heard them. They expressed their surprise. The Englishman had never quitted the hall; it was said he smiled with a most particular and extraordinary expression as the remark was made. His silence had been noticed before, but it was ascribed to his ignorance of the

Spanish language, an ignorance that Spaniards are not anxious either to expose or remove by speaking to a stranger. The subject of the music was not again reverted to till the guests were seated at supper, when Donna Ines and her young husband, exchanging a smile of delighted surprise, exclaimed they heard the same delicious sounds floating round them. The guests listened, but no one else could hear it;—everyone felt there was something extraordinary in this. Hush! was uttered by every voice almost at the same moment. A dead silence followed,—you would think, from their intent looks, that they listened with their very eyes. This deep silence, contrasted with the splendor of the feast, and the light effused from torches held by the domestics, produced a singular effect,—it seemed for some moments like an assembly of the dead. The silence was interrupted, though the cause of wonder had not ceased, by the entrance of Father Olavida, the Confessor of Donna Isabella, who had been called away previous to the feast, to administer extreme unction to a dying man in the neighborhood. He was a priest of uncommon sanctity, beloved in the family, and respected in the neighborhood, where he had displayed uncommon taste and talents for exorcism;—in fact, this was the good Father's forte, and he piqued himself on it accordingly. The devil never fell into worse hands than Father Olavida's, for when he was so contumacious as to resist Latin, and even the first verses of the Gospel of St. John in Greek, which the good Father never had recourse to but in cases of extreme stubbornness and difficulty,— (here Stanton recollected the English story of the Boy of

Bilson, and blushed even in Spain for his countrymen),—then he always applied to the Inquisition; and if the devils were ever so obstinate before, they were always seen to fly out of the possessed, just as, in the midst of their cries (no doubt of blasphemy), they were tied to the stake. Some held out even till the flames surrounded them; but even the most stubborn must have been dislodged when the operation was over, for the devil himself could no longer tenant a crisp and glutinous lump of cinders. Thus Father Olavida's fame spread far and wide, and the Cardoza family had made uncommon interest to procure him for a Confessor, and happily succeeded. The ceremony he had just been performing had cast a shade over the good Father's countenance, but it dispersed as he mingled among the guests, and was introduced to them. Room was soon made for him, and he happened accidentally to be seated opposite the Englishman. As the wine was presented to him, Father Olavida (who, as I observed, was a man of singular sanctity) prepared to utter a short internal prayer. He hesitated,— trembled,—desisted; and, putting down the wine, wiped the drops from his forehead with the sleeve of his habit. Donna Isabella gave a sign to a domestic, and other wine of a higher quality was offered to him. His lips moved, as if in the effort to pronounce a benediction on it and the company, but the effort again failed; and the change in his countenance was so extraordinary, that it was perceived by all the guests. He felt the sensation that his extraordinary appearance excited, and attempted to remove it by again endeavoring to lift the cup to his lips. So strong was the anxiety with which the company watched him, that the only sound heard in that spacious and crowded hall was the rustling of his habit as he attempted to lift the cup to his lips once more—in vain. The guests sat in astonished silence. Father Olavida alone remained standing; but at that moment the Englishman rose, and appeared determined to fix Olavida's regards by a gaze like that of fascination. Olavida rocked, reeled, grasped the arm of a page, and at last, closing his eyes for a moment, as if to escape the horrible fascination of that unearthly glare (the Englishman's eyes were observed by all the guests, from the moment of his entrance, to effuse a most fearful and preternatural luster), exclaimed, "Who is among us?—Who?—I cannot utter a blessing while he is here. I cannot feel one. Where he treads, the earth is parched!—Where he breathes, the air is fire!—Where he feeds, the food is poison!— Where he turns his glance is lightning!—WHO IS AMONG US?—WHO?" repeated the priest in the agony of adjuration, while his cowl fallen back, his few thin hairs around the scalp instinct and alive with terrible emotion, his outspread arms protruded from the sleeves of his habit, and extended toward the awful stranger, suggested the idea of an inspired being in the dreadful rapture of prophetic denunciation. He stood—still stood, and the Englishman stood calmly opposite to him. There was an agitated irregularity in the attitudes of those around them, which contrasted strongly the fixed and stern postures of those two, who remained gazing silently at each other. "Who knows him?" exclaimed Olavida, starting apparently from a trance; "who knows him? who brought him here?"

The guests severally disclaimed all knowledge of the Englishman, and each asked the other in whispers, "who HAD brought him there?" Father Olavida then pointed his arm to each of the company, and asked each individually, "Do you know him?" No! no! no!" was uttered with vehement emphasis by every individual. "But I know him," said Olavida, "by these cold drops!" and he wiped them off;— "by these convulsed joints!" and he attempted to sign the cross, but could not. He raised his voice, and evidently speaking with increased difficulty,—"By this bread and wine, which the faithful receive as the body and blood of Christ, but which HIS presence converts into matter as viperous as the suicide foam of the dying Judas,—by all these—I know him, and command him to be gone!—He is—he is—" and he bent forward as he spoke, and gazed on the Englishman with an expression which the mixture of rage, hatred, and fear rendered terrible. All the guests rose at these words,— the whole company now presented two singular groups, that of the amazed guests all collected together, and repeating,

"Who, what is he?" and that of the Englishman, who stood unmoved, and Olavida, who dropped dead in the attitude of pointing to him.

..... .

The body was removed into another room, and the departure of the Englishman was not noticed till the company returned to the hall. They sat late together, conversing on this extraordinary circumstance, and finally agreed to remain in the house, lest the evil spirit (for they believed the Englishman no better) should take certain liberties with the corse by no means agreeable to a Catholic, particularly as he had manifestly died without the benefit of the last sacraments. Just as this laudable resolution was formed, they were roused by cries of horror and agony from the bridal chamber, where the young pair had retired.

They hurried to the door, but the father was first. They burst it open, and found the bride a corse in the arms of her husband.

..... .

He never recovered his reason; the family deserted the mansion rendered terrible by so many misfortunes. One apartment is still tenanted by the unhappy maniac; his were the cries you heard as you traversed the deserted rooms. He is for the most part silent during the day, but at midnight he always exclaims, in a voice frightfully piercing, and hardly human, "They are coming! they are coming!" and relapses into profound silence.

The funeral of Father Olavida was attended by an extraordinary circumstance. He was interred in a neighboring convent; and the reputation of his sanctity, joined to the interest caused by his

corse, as it lay before them cold and motionless, every eye was fixed, and every ear became attentive. Even the lovers, who, under pretense of dipping their fingers into the holy water, were contriving to exchange amorous billets, forbore for one moment this interesting intercourse, to listen to the preacher. He dwelt with much energy on the virtues of the deceased, whom he declared to be a particular favorite of the Virgin; and enumerating the various losses that would be caused by his departure to the community to which he belonged, to society, and to religion at large; he at last worked up himself to a vehement expostulation with the Deity on the occasion. "Why hast thou," he exclaimed, "why hast thou, Oh God! thus dealt with us? Why hast thou snatched from our sight this glorious saint, whose merits, if properly applied, doubtless would have been sufficient to atone for the apostasy of St. Peter, the opposition of St. Paul (previous to his conversion), and even the treachery of Judas himself? Why hast thou, Oh God! snatched him from us?"—and a deep and hollow voice from among the congregation extraordinary death, collected vast numbers at the ceremony. His funeral sermon was preached by a monk of distinguished eloquence, appointed for the purpose. To render the effect of his discourse more powerful, the corse, extended on a bier, with its face uncovered, was placed in the aisle. The monk took his text from one of the prophets,—"Death is gone up into our palaces." He expatiated on mortality, whose approach, whether abrupt or lingering, is alike awful to man.—He spoke of the vicisstudes of empires with much eloquence and learning, but his audience were not observed to be much affected.—He cited various passages from the lives of the saints, descriptive of the glories of martyrdom, and the heroism of those who had bled and blazed for Christ and his blessed mother, but they appeared still waiting for something to touch them more deeply. When he inveighed against the tyrants under whose bloody persecution those holy men suffered, his hearers were roused for a moment, for it is always easier to excite a passion than a moral feeling. But when he spoke of the dead, and pointed with emphatic gesture to the answered,—"Because he deserved his fate." The murmurs of approbation with which the congregation honored this apostrophe half drowned this extraordinary interruption; and though there was some little commotion in the immediate vicinity of the speaker, the rest of the audience continued to listen intently. "What," proceeded the preacher, pointing to the corse, "what hath laid thee there, servant of God?"—"Pride, ignorance, and fear," answered the same voice, in accents still more thrilling. The disturbance now became universal. The preacher paused, and a circle opening, disclosed the figure of a monk belonging to the convent, who stood among them.

.. . ..

After all the usual modes of admonition, exhortation, and discipline had been employed, and the bishop of the diocese, who, under the report of these extraordinary circumstances, had visited the convent in person to obtain some explanation from the contumacious monk in vain, it was agreed, in a chapter extraordinary, to surrender him to the power of the Inquisition. He testified great horror when this determination was made known to him, —and offered to tell over and over again all that he COULD relate of the cause of Father Olavida's death. His humiliation, and repeated offers of confession, came too late. He was conveyed to the Inquisition. The proceedings of that tribunal are rarely disclosed, but there is a secret report (I cannot answer for its truth) of what he said and suffered there. On his first examination, he said he would relate all he COULD. He was told that was not enough, he must relate all he knew.

. . . . .

"Why did you testify such horror at the funeral of Father Olavida?"—"Everyone testified horror and grief at the death of that venerable ecclesiastic, who died in the odor of sanctity. Had I done otherwise, it might have been reckoned a proof of my guilt." "Why did you interrupt the preacher with such extraordinary exclamations?"—To this no answer. "Why do you refuse to explain the meaning of those exclamations?"—No answer. "Why do you persist in this obstinate and dangerous silence? Look, I beseech you, brother, at the cross that is suspended against this wall," and the Inquisitor pointed to the large black crucifix at the back of the chair where he sat; "one drop of the blood shed there can purify you from all the sin you have ever committed; but all that blood, combined with the intercession of the Queen of Heaven, and the merits of all its martyrs, nay, even the absolution of the Pope, cannot deliver you from the curse of dying in unrepented sin."—"What sin, then, have I committed?"—"The greatest of all possible sins; you refuse answering the questions put to you at the tribunal of the most holy and merciful Inquisition;—you will not tell us what you know concerning the death of Father Olavida."—"I have told you that I believe he perished in consequence of his ignorance and presumption." "What proof can you produce of that?"— "He sought the knowledge of a secret withheld from man." "What was that?"—"The secret of discovering the presence or agency of the evil power." "Do you possess that secret?"—After much agitation on the part of the prisoner, he said distinctly, but very faintly, "My master forbids me to disclose it." "If your master were Jesus Christ, he would not forbid you to obey the commands, or answer the questions of the Inquisition."—"I am not sure of that." There was a general outcry of horror at these words. The examination then went on. "If you believed Olavida to be guilty of any pursuits or studies condemned by our mother the church, why did you not denounce him to the Inquisition?"—"Because I believed him not likely to be injured by such pursuits; his mind was too weak,— he died in the struggle," said the prisoner with great emphasis. "You believe, then, it requires strength of mind to keep those abominable secrets, when examined as to their nature and tendency?"—"No, I rather imagine strength of body." "We shall try that presently," said an Inquisitor, giving a signal for the torture.

… . .

The prisoner underwent the first and second applications with unshrinking courage, but on the infliction of the water-torture, which is indeed insupportable to humanity, either to suffer or relate, he exclaimed in the gasping interval, he would disclose everything. He was released, refreshed, restored, and the following day uttered the following remarkable confession... .

. . . . .

The old Spanish woman further confessed to Stanton, that... .

. . . . .

and that the Englishman certainly had been seen in the neighborhood since;—seen, as she had heard, that very night. "Great G—d!" exclaimed Stanton, as he recollected the stranger whose demoniac laugh had so appalled him, while gazing on the lifeless bodies of the lovers, whom the lightning had struck and blasted.

As the manuscript, after a few blotted and illegible pages, became more distinct, Melmoth read on, perplexed and unsatisfied, not knowing what connection this Spanish story could have with his ancestor, whom, however, he recognized under the title of the Englishman; and wondering how Stanton could have thought it worth his while to follow him to Ireland, write a long manuscript about an event that occurred in Spain, and leave it in the hands of his family, to "verify untrue things," in the language of Dogberry,— his wonder was diminished, though his curiosity was still more inflamed, by the perusal of the next lines, which he made out with some difficulty. It seems Stanton was now in England.

. . . . .

About the year 1677, Stanton was in London, his mind still full of his mysterious countryman. This

constant subject of his contemplations had produced a visible change in his exterior,—his walk was what Sallust tells us of Catiline's,—his were, too, the "faedi oculi." He said to himself every moment, "If I could but trace that being, I will not call him man,"—and the next moment he said, "and what if I could?" In this state of mind, it is singular enough that he mixed constantly in public amusements, but it is true. When one fierce passion is devouring the soul, we feel more than ever the necessity of external excitement; and our dependence on the world for temporary relief increases in direct proportion to our contempt of the world and all its works. He went frequently to the theaters, THEN fashionable, when

"The fair sat panting at a courtier's play,
And not a mask went unimproved away."

. . . . .

It was that memorable night, when, according to the history of the veteran Betterton,[1] Mrs. Barry, who personated Roxana, had a green-room squabble with Mrs. Bowtell, the representative of Statira, about a veil, which the partiality of the property man adjudged to the latter. Roxana suppressed her rage till the fifth act, when, stabbing

Statira, she aimed the blow with such force as to pierce through her stays, and inflict a severe though not dangerous wound. Mrs. Bowtell fainted, the performance was suspended, and, in the commotion which this incident caused in the house, many of the audience rose, and Stanton among them. It was at this moment that, in a seat opposite to him, he discovered the object of his search for four years,— the Englishman whom he had met in the plains of Valencia, and whom he believed the same with the subject of the extraordinary narrative he had heard there.

He was standing up. There was nothing particular or remarkable in his appearance, but the expression of his eyes could never be mistaken or forgotten. The heart of Stanton palpitated with violence,—a mist overspread his eye,—a nameless and deadly sickness, accompanied with a creeping sensation in every pore, from which cold drops were gushing, announced the... .

. . . . .

Before he had well recovered, a strain of music, soft, solemn, and delicious, breathed round him, audibly ascending from the ground, and increasing in sweetness and power till it seemed to fill the whole building. Under the sudden impulse of amazement and pleasure, he inquired of some around him from whence those exquisite sounds arose. But, by the manner in which he was answered, it was plain that those he addressed considered him insane; and, indeed, the remarkable change in his expression might well justify the suspicion. He then remembered that night in Spain, when the same sweet and mysterious sounds were heard only by the young bridegroom and bride, of whom the latter perished on that very night. "And am I then to be the next victim?" thought Stanton; "and are those celestial sounds, that seem to prepare us for heaven, only intended to announce the presence of an incarnate fiend, who mocks the devoted with 'airs from heaven,' while he prepares to surround them with 'blasts from hell'?" It is very singular that at this moment, when his imagination had reached its highest pitch of elevation,—when the object he had pursued so long and fruitlessly, had in one moment become as it were tangible to the grasp both of mind and body,—when this spirit, with whom he had wrestled in darkness, was at last about to declare its name, that Stanton began to feel a kind of disappointment at the futility of his pursuits, like Bruce at discovering the source of the Nile, or Gibbon on concluding his History. The feeling which he had dwelt on so long, that he had actually converted it into a duty, was after all mere curiosity; but what passion is more insatiable, or more capable of giving a kind of romantic grandeur to all its wanderings and eccentricities? Curiosity is in one respect like love, it always compromises between the object and the feeling; and provided the latter possesses sufficient energy, no matter how contemptible the former may be. A child might have smiled at the agitation of Stanton, caused as it was by the accidental appearance of a stranger; but no man, in the full energy of his passions, was there, but must have trembled at the horrible agony of emotion with which he felt approaching, with sudden and irresistible velocity, the crisis of his destiny.

When the play was over, he stood for some

moments in the deserted streets. It was a beautiful moonlight night, and he saw near him a figure, whose shadow, projected half across the street (there were no flagged ways then, chains and posts were the only defense of the foot passenger), appeared to him of gigantic magnitude. He had been so long accustomed to contend with these phantoms of the imagination, that he took a kind of stubborn delight in subduing them. He walked up to the object, and observing the shadow only was magnified, and the figure was the ordinary height of man, he approached it, and discovered the very object of his search,—the man whom he had seen for a moment in Valencia, and, after a search of four years, recognized at the theater.

. . . . .

"You were in quest of me?"—"I was." "Have you anything to inquire of me?"—"Much." "Speak, then."—"This is no place." "No place! poor wretch, I am independent of time and place. Speak, if you have anything to ask or to learn."—"I have many things to ask, but nothing to learn, I hope, from you." "You deceive yourself, but you will be undeceived when next we meet."—"And when shall that be?" said Stanton, grasping his arm; "name your hour and your place." "The hour shall be midday," answered the stranger, with a horrid and unintelligible smile; "and the place shall be the bare walls of a madhouse, where you shall rise rattling in your chains, and rustling from your straw, to greet me,—yet still you shall have THE CURSE OF SANITY, and of memory. My voice shall ring in your ears till then, and the glance of these eyes shall be reflected from every object, animate or inanimate, till you behold them again."—"Is it under circumstances so horrible we are to meet again?" said Stanton, shrinking under the full-lighted blaze of those demon eyes. "I never," said the stranger, in an emphatic tone,—"I never desert my friends in misfortune. When they are plunged in the lowest abyss of human calamity, they are sure to be visited by me."

. . . . .

The narrative, when Melmoth was again able to trace its continuation, described Stanton, some years after, plunged in a state the most deplorable.

He had been always reckoned of a singular turn of mind, and the belief of this, aggravated by his constant talk of Melmoth, his wild pursuit of him, his strange behavior at the theater, and his dwelling on the various particulars of their extraordinary meetings, with all the intensity of the deepest conviction (while he never could impress them on any one's conviction but his own), suggested to some prudent people the idea that he was deranged. Their malignity probably took part with their prudence. The selfish Frenchman[2] says, we feel a pleasure even in the misfortunes of our friends,—a plus forte in those of our enemies; and as everyone is an enemy to a man of genius of course, the report of Stanton's malady was propagated with infernal and successful industry. Stanton's next relative, a needy unprincipled man, watched the report in its circulation, and saw the snares closing round his victim. He waited on him one morning, accompanied by a person of a grave, though somewhat repulsive appearance. Stanton was as usual abstracted and restless, and, after a few moments' conversation, he proposed a drive a few miles out of London, which he said would revive and refresh him. Stanton objected, on account of the difficulty of getting a hackney coach (for it is singular that at this period the number of private equipages, though infinitely fewer than they are now, exceeded the number of hired ones), and proposed going by water. This, however, did not suit the kinsman's views; and, after pretending to send for a carriage (which was in waiting at the end of the street), Stanton and his companions entered it, and drove about two miles out of London.

The carriage then stopped. Come, Cousin," said the younger Stanton,—"come and view a purchase I have made." Stanton absently alighted, and followed him across a small paved court; the other person followed. "In troth, Cousin," said Stanton, "your choice appears not to have been discreetly made; your house has somewhat of a gloomy aspect."—"Hold you content, Cousin," replied the other; "I shall take order that you like it better, when you have been some time a dweller therein." Some attendants of a mean appearance, and with most suspicious visages, awaited them on their entrance, and they ascended a narrow staircase, which led to a room meanly furnished. "Wait here," said the kinsman, to the man who accompanied them, "till I go for company to divertise my cousin in his loneliness." They were left alone. Stanton took no notice of his companion, but as usual seized the first book near him, and began to read. It was a volume in manuscript,—they were then much more common than now.

The first lines struck him as indicating insanity in the writer. It was a wild proposal (written apparently after the great fire of London) to rebuild it with stone, and attempting to prove, on a calculation wild, false, and yet sometimes plausible, that this could be done out of the colossal fragments of Stonehenge, which the writer proposed to remove for that purpose. Subjoined were several grotesque drawings of engines designed to remove those massive blocks, and in a corner of the page was a note,—"I would have drawn these more accurately, but was not allowed a KNIFE to mend my pen."

The next was entitled, "A modest proposal for the spreading of Christianity in foreign parts, whereby it is hoped its entertainment will become general all over the world."—This modest proposal was, to convert the Turkish ambassadors (who had been in London a few years before), by offering them their choice of being strangled on the spot, or becoming Christians. Of course the writer reckoned on their embracing the easier alternative, but even this was to be clogged with a heavy condition,—namely, that they must be bound before a magistrate to convert twenty Mussulmans a day, on their return to Turkey. The rest of the pamphlet was reasoned very much in the conclusive style of Captain Bobadil,— these twenty will convert twenty more apiece, and these two hundred converts, converting their due number in the same time, all Turkey would be converted before the Grand Signior knew where he was. Then comes the coup d'eclat,—one fine morning, every minaret in Constantinople was to ring out with bells, instead of the cry of the Muezzins; and the Imaum, coming out to see what was the matter, was to be encountered by the Archbishop of Canterbury, in pontificalibus, performing Cathedral service in the church of St. Sophia, which was to finish the business. Here an objection appeared to arise, which the ingenuity of the writer had anticipated.—"It may be redargued," saith he, "by those who have more spleen than brain, that forasmuch as the Archbishop preacheth in English, he will not thereby much edify the Turkish folk, who do altogether hold in a vain gabble of their own." But this (to use his own language) he "evites," by judiciously observing, that where service was performed in an unknown tongue, the devotion of the people was always observed to be much increased thereby; as, for instance, in the church of Rome,—that St. Augustine, with his monks, advanced to meet King Ethelbert singing litanies (in a language his majesty could not possibly have understood), and converted him and his whole court on the spot;—that the sybilline books... .

..... .

Cum multis aliis.

Between the pages were cut most exquisitely in paper the likenesses of some of these Turkish ambassadors; the hair of the beards, in particular, was feathered with a delicacy of touch that seemed the work of fairy fingers,—but the pages ended with a complaint of the operator, that his scissors had been taken from him. However, he consoled himself and the reader with the assurance, that he would that night catch a moonbeam as it entered through the grating, and, when he had whetted it on the iron knobs of his door, would do wonders with it. In the next page was found a melancholy proof of powerful but prostrated intellect. It contained some insane lines, ascribed to Lee the dramatic poet, commencing,

"O that my lungs could bleat like buttered pease," &c.

There is no proof whatever that these miserable lines were really written by Lee, except that the measure is the fashionable quatrain of the period. It is singular that Stanton read on without suspicion of his own danger, quite absorbed in the album of a madhouse, without ever reflecting on the place where he was, and which such compositions too manifestly designated.

It was after a long interval that he looked round, and perceived that his companion was gone. Bells were unusual then. He proceeded to the door,—it was fastened. He called aloud,—his voice was echoed in a moment by many others, but in tones so wild and discordant, that he desisted in involuntary terror. As the day advanced, and no one approached, he tried the window, and then perceived for the first time it was grated. It looked out on the narrow flagged yard, in which no human being was; and if there had, from such a being no human feeling could have been extracted.

Sickening with unspeakable horror, he sunk rather than sat down beside the miserable window, and "wished for day."

. . . . .

At midnight he started from a doze, half a swoon, half a sleep, which probably the hardness of his seat, and of the deal table on which he leaned, had not contributed to prolong.

He was in complete darkness; the horror of his situation struck him at once, and for a moment he was indeed almost qualified for an inmate of that dreadful mansion. He felt his way to the door, shook it with desperate strength, and uttered the most frightful cries, mixed with expostulations and commands. His cries were in a moment echoed by a hundred voices. In maniacs there is a peculiar malignity, accompanied by an extraordinary acuteness of some of the senses, particularly in distinguishing the voice of a stranger. The cries that he heard on every side seemed like a wild and infernal yell of joy, that their mansion of misery had obtained another tenant.

He paused, exhausted,—a quick and thundering step was heard in the passage. The door was opened, and a man of savage appearance stood at the entrance,—two more were seen indistinctly in the passage. "Release me, villain!"—"Stop, my fine fellow, what's all this noise for?" "Where am I?" "Where you ought to be." "Will you dare to detain me?"—"Yes, and a little more than that," answered the ruffian, applying a loaded horsewhip to his back and shoulders, till the patient soon fell to the ground convulsed with rage and pain. "Now you see you are where you ought to be," repeated the ruffian, brandishing the horsewhip over him, "and now take the advice of a friend, and make no more noise. The lads are ready for you with the darbies, and they'll clink them on in the crack of this whip, unless you prefer another touch of it first." They then were advancing into the room as he spoke, with fetters in their hands (strait waistcoats being then little known or used), and showed, by their frightful countenances and gestures, no unwillingness to apply them. Their harsh rattle on the stone pavement made Stanton's blood run cold; the effect, however, was useful. He had the presence of mind to acknowledge his (supposed) miserable condition, to supplicate the forbearance of the ruthless keeper, and promise complete submission to his orders. This pacified the ruffian, and he retired.

Stanton collected all his resolution to encounter the horrible night; he saw all that was before him, and summoned himself to meet it. After much agitated deliberation, he conceived it best to continue the same appearance of submission and tranquillity, hoping that thus he might in time either propitiate the wretches in whose hands he was, or, by his apparent inoffensiveness, procure such opportunities of indulgence, as might perhaps ultimately facilitate his escape. He therefore determined to conduct himself with the utmost tranquillity, and never to let his voice be heard in the house; and he laid down several other resolutions with a degree of prudence which he already shuddered to think might be the cunning of incipient madness, or the beginning result of the horrid habits of the place.

These resolutions were put to desperate trial that very night. Just next to Stanton's apartment were lodged two most uncongenial neighbors. One of them was a puritanical weaver, who had been driven mad by a single sermon from the celebrated Hugh Peters, and was sent to the madhouse as full of election and reprobation as he could hold,—and fuller. He regularly repeated over the five points while daylight lasted, and imagined himself preaching in a conventicle with distinguished success; toward twilight his visions were more gloomy, and at midnight his blasphemies became horrible. In the opposite cell was lodged a loyalist tailor, who had been ruined by giving credit to the cavaliers and their ladies,—(for at this time, and much later, down to the reign of Anne, tailors were employed by females even to make and fit on their stays),—who had run mad with drink and loyalty on the burning of the Rump, and ever since had made the cells of the madhouse echo with fragments of the ill-fated Colonel Lovelace's song, scraps from Cowley's "Cutter of Coleman street," and some curious specimens from Mrs. Aphra Behn's plays, where the cavaliers are denominated the heroicks, and Lady Lambert and Lady Desborough represented as going to meeting, their large Bibles carried before them by their pages, and falling in love with two banished cavaliers by the way. The voice in which he shrieked out such words was powerfully horrible, but it was like the moan of an infant compared to the voice which took up and reechoed the cry, in a tone that made the building shake. It was the voice of a maniac, who had lost her husband, children, subsistence, and finally her reason, in the dreadful fire of London. The cry of fire never failed to operate with terrible punctuality on her associations. She had been in a disturbed sleep, and now started from it as suddenly as on that dreadful night. It was Saturday night too, and she was always observed to be particularly violent on that night,—it was the terrible weekly festival of insanity with her. She was awake, and busy in a moment escaping from the flames; and she dramatized the whole scene with such hideous fidelity, that Stanton's resolution was far more in danger from her than from the battle between his neighbors Testimony and Hothead. She began exclaiming she was suffocated by the smoke; then she sprung from her bed, calling for a light, and appeared to be struck by the sudden glare that burst through her casement.—"The last day," she shrieked, "The last day! The very heavens are on fire!"—"That will not come till the Man of Sin be first destroyed," cried the weaver; "thou ravest of light and fire, and yet thou art in utter darkness.—I pity thee, poor mad soul, I pity thee!" The maniac never heeded him; she appeared to be scrambling up a staircase to her children's room. She exclaimed she was scorched, singed, suffocated; her courage appeared to fail, and she retreated. "But my children are there!" she cried in a voice of unspeakable agony, as she seemed to make another effort; "here I am—here I am come to save you.—Oh God! They are all blazing!—Take this arm—no, not that, it is scorched and disabled — well, any arm—take hold of my clothes—no, they are blazing too!— Well, take me all on fire as I am!—And their hair, how it hisses!—Water, one drop of water for my youngest—he is but an infant —for my youngest, and let me burn!" She paused in horrid silence, to watch the fall of a blazing rafter that was about to shatter the staircase on which she stood.—"The roof has fallen on my head!" she exclaimed. "The earth is weak, and all the inhabitants thereof," chanted the weaver; "I bear up the pillars of it."

The maniac marked the destruction of the spot where she thought she stood by one desperate bound, accompanied by a wild shriek, and then calmly gazed on her infants as they rolled over the scorching fragments, and sunk into the abyss of fire below. "There they go,— one—two—three—all!" and her voice sunk into low mutterings, and her convulsions into faint, cold shudderings, like the sobbings of a spent storm, as she imagined herself to "stand in safety and despair," amid the thousand houseless wretches assembled in the suburbs of London on the dreadful nights after the fire, without food, roof, or raiment, all gazing on the burning ruins of their dwellings and their property. She seemed to listen to their complaints, and even repeated some of them very affectingly, but invariably answered them with the same words, "But I have lost all my children—all!" It was remarkable, that when this sufferer began to rave, all the others became silent. The cry of nature hushed every other cry,—she was the only patient in the house who was not mad from politics, religion, ebriety, or some perverted passion; and terrifying as the outbreak of her frenzy always was, Stanton used to await it as a kind of relief from the dissonant, melancholy, and ludicrous ravings of the others.

But the utmost efforts of his resolution began to sink under the continued horrors of the place. The impression on his senses began to defy the power of reason to resist them. He could not shut out these frightful cries nightly repeated, nor the frightful sound of the whip employed to still them. Hope began to fail him, as he observed, that the submissive tranquillity (which he had imagined, by obtaining increased indulgence, might contribute to his escape, or perhaps convince the keeper of his sanity) was interpreted by the callous ruffian, who was acquainted only with the varieties of MADNESS, as a more refined species of that cunning which he was well accustomed to watch and baffle.

On his first discovery of his situation, he had determined to take the utmost care of his health and intellect that the place allowed, as the sole basis of his hope of deliverance. But as that hope declined, he neglected the means of realizing it. He had at first risen early, walked incessantly about his cell, and availed himself of every opportunity of being in the open air. He took the strictest care of his person in point of cleanliness, and with or without appetite, regularly forced down his miserable meals; and all these efforts were even pleasant, as long as hope prompted them. But now he began to relax them all. He passed half the day in his wretched bed, in which he frequently took his meals, declined shaving or changing his linen, and, when the sun shone into his cell, he turned from it on his straw with a sigh of heartbroken despondency. Formerly, when the air breathed through his grating, he used to say, "Blessed air of heaven, I shall breathe you once more in freedom! —Reserve all your freshness for that delicious evening when I shall inhale you, and be as free as you myself." Now when he felt it, he sighed and said nothing. The twitter of the sparrows, the pattering of rain, or the moan of the wind, sounds that he used to sit up in his bed to catch with delight, as reminding him of nature, were now unheeded.

He began at times to listen with sullen and horrible pleasure to the cries of his miserable companions. He became squalid, listless, torpid, and disgusting in his appearance.

. . . . .

It was one of those dismal nights, that, as he tossed on his loathsome bed,—more loathsome from the impossibility to quit it without feeling more "unrest,"—he perceived the miserable light that burned in the hearth was obscured by the intervention of some dark object. He turned feebly toward the light, without curiosity, without excitement, but with a wish to diversify the monotony of his misery, by observing the slightest change made even accidentally in the dusky atmosphere of his cell. Between him and the light stood the figure of Melmoth, just as he had seen him from the first; the figure was the same; the expression of the face was the same,—cold, stony, and rigid; the eyes, with their infernal and dazzling luster, were still the same.

Stanton's ruling passion rushed on his soul; he felt this apparition like a summons to a high and fearful encounter. He heard his heart beat audibly, and could have exclaimed with Lee's unfortunate heroine,—"It pants as cowards do before a battle;

Oh the great march has sounded!"

Melmoth approached him with that frightful calmness that mocks the terror it excites. "My prophecy has been fulfilled;—you rise to meet me rattling from your chains, and rustling from your straw—am I not a true prophet?" Stanton was silent. "Is not your situation very miserable?"—Still Stanton was silent; for he was beginning to believe this an illusion of madness. He thought to himself, "How could he have gained entrance here?"—"Would you not wish to be delivered from it?" Stanton tossed on his straw, and its rustling seemed to answer the question. "I have the power to deliver you from it." Melmoth spoke very slowly and very softly, and the melodious smoothness of his voice made a frightful contrast to the stony rigor of his features, and the fiendlike brilliancy of his eyes. "Who are you, and whence come you?" said Stanton, in a tone that was meant to be interrogatory and imperative, but which, from his habits of squalid debility, was at once feeble and querulous. His intellect had become affected by the gloom of his miserable habitation, as the wretched inmate of a similar mansion, when produced before a medical examiner, was reported to be a complete Albino.—His skin was bleached, his eyes turned white; he could not bear the light; and, when exposed to it, he turned away with a mixture of weakness and restlessness, more like the writhings of a sick infant than the struggles of a man.

Such was Stanton's situation. He was enfeebled now, and the power of the enemy seemed without a possibility of opposition from either his intellectual or corporeal powers.

. . . . .

Of all their horrible dialogue, only these words were legible in the manuscript, "You know me now."—"I always knew you."—"That is false; you imagined you did, and that has been the cause of all the wild . of the … … of your finally being lodged in this mansion of misery, where only I would seek, where only I can succor you."—"You, demon!"—"Demon!—Harsh words!—Was it a demon or a human being placed you here?—Listen to me, Stanton; nay, wrap not yourself in that miserable blanket,—that cannot shut out my words. Believe

me, were you folded in thunder clouds, you must hear ME! Stanton, think of your misery. These bare walls—what do they present to the intellect or to the senses?—Whitewash, diversified with the scrawls of charcoal or red chalk, that your happy predecessors have left for you to trace over. You have a taste for drawing—I trust it will improve. And here's a grating, through which the sun squints on you like a stepdame, and the breeze blows, as if it meant to tantalize you with a sigh from that sweet mouth, whose kiss you must never enjoy. And where's your library,—intellectual man,—traveled man?" he repeated in a tone of bitter derision; "where be your companions, your peaked men of countries, as your favorite Shakespeare has it? You must be content with the spider and the rat, to crawl and scratch round your flock bed! I have known prisoners in the Bastille to feed them for companions,—why don't you begin your task? I have known a spider to descend at the tap of a finger, and a rat to come forth when the daily meal was brought, to share it with his fellow prisoner!— How delightful to have vermin for your guests! Aye, and when the feast fails them, they make a meal of their entertainer!—You shudder.—Are you, then, the first prisoner who has been devoured alive by the vermin that infested his cell?—Delightful banquet, not 'where you eat, but where you are eaten'! Your guests, however, will give you one token of repentance while they feed; there will be gnashing of teeth, and you shall hear it, and feel it too perchance!—And then for meals—Oh you are daintily off!—The soup that the cat has lapped; and (as her progeny has probably contributed to the hell broth) why not? Then your hours of solitude, deliciously diversified by the yell of famine, the howl of madness, the crash of whips, and the broken-hearted sob of those who, like you, are supposed, or DRIVEN mad by the crimes of others!—Stanton, do you imagine your reason can possibly hold out amid such scenes?— Supposing your reason was unimpaired, your health not destroyed,— suppose all this, which is, after all, more than fair supposition can grant, guess the effect of the continuance of these scenes on your senses alone. A time will come, and soon, when, from mere habit, you will echo the scream of every delirious wretch that harbors near you; then you will pause, clasp your hands on your throbbing head, and listen with horrible anxiety whether the scream proceeded from YOU or THEM. The time will come, when, from the want of occupation, the listless and horrible vacancy of your hours, you will feel as anxious to hear those shrieks, as you were at first terrified to hear them,—when you will watch for the ravings of your next neighbor, as you would for a scene on the stage. All humanity will be extinguished in you. The ravings of these wretches will become at once your sport and your torture. You will watch for the sounds, to mock them with the grimaces and bellowings of a fiend. The mind has a power of accommodating itself to its situation, that you will experience in its most frightful and deplorable efficacy. Then comes the dreadful doubt of one's own sanity, the terrible announcer that THAT doubt will soon become fear, and THAT fear certainty. Perhaps (still more dreadful) the FEAR will at last become a HOPE,— shut out from society, watched by a brutal keeper, writhing with all the impotent agony of an incarcerated mind, without communication and without sympathy, unable to exchange ideas but with those whose ideas are only the hideous specters of departed intellect, or even to hear the welcome sound of the human voice, except to mistake it for the howl of a fiend, and stop the ear desecrated by its intrusion,— then at last your fear will become a more fearful hope; you will wish to become one of them, to escape the agony of consciousness. As those who have long leaned over a precipice, have at last felt a desire to plunge below, to relieve the intolerable temptation of their giddiness,[3] you will hear them laugh amid their wildest paroxysms; you will say, 'Doubtless those wretches have some consolation, but I have none; my sanity is my greatest curse in this abode of horrors. They greedily devour their miserable meals, while I loathe mine. They sleep sometimes soundly, while my sleep is—worse than their waking. They are revived every morning by some delicious illusion of cunning madness, soothing them with the hope of escaping, baffling or tormenting their keeper; my sanity precludes all such hope. I KNOW I NEVER CAN ESCAPE, and the preservation of my faculties is only an aggravation of my sufferings. I have all their miseries,—I have none of their consolations. They laugh,—I hear them; would I could laugh like them.' You will try, and the very effort will be an invocation to the demon of insanity to come and take full possession of you from that moment forever."

(There were other details, both of the menaces and

temptations employed by Melmoth, which are too horrible for insertion. One of them may serve for an instance.)

"You think that the intellectual power is something distinct from the vitality of the soul, or, in other words, that if even your reason should be destroyed (which it nearly is), your soul might yet enjoy beatitude in the full exercise of its enlarged and exalted faculties, and all the clouds which obscured them be dispelled by the Sun of Righteousness, in whose beams you hope to bask forever and ever. Now, without going into any metaphysical subtleties about the distinction between mind and soul, experience must teach you, that there can be no crime into which madmen would not, and do not, precipitate themselves; mischief is their occupation, malice their habit, murder their sport, and blasphemy their delight. Whether a soul in this state can be in a hopeful one, it is for you to judge; but it seems to me, that with the loss of reason (and reason cannot long be retained in this place) you lose also the hope of immortality.—Listen," said the tempter, pausing, "listen to the wretch who is raving near you, and whose blasphemies might make a demon start.—He was once an eminent puritanical preacher. Half the day he imagines himself in a pulpit, denouncing damnation against Papists, Arminians, and even Sublapsarians (he being a Supra-lapsarian himself). He foams, he writhes, he gnashes his teeth; you would imagine him in the hell he was painting, and that the fire and brimstone he is so lavish of were actually exhaling from his jaws. At night his creed retaliates on him; he believes himself one of the reprobates he has been all day denouncing, and curses God for the very decree he has all day been glorifying Him for.

"He, whom he has for twelve hours been vociferating 'is the loveliest among ten thousand,' becomes the object of demoniac hostility and execration. He grapples with the iron posts of his bed, and says he is rooting out the cross from the very foundations of Calvary; and it is remarkable, that in proportion as his morning exercises are intense, vivid, and eloquent, his nightly blasphemies are outrageous and horrible.—Hark!

Now he believes himself a demon; listen to his diabolical eloquence of horror!"

Stanton listened, and shuddered . .

.. . . .

"Escape—escape for your life," cried the tempter; "break forth into life, liberty, and sanity. Your social happiness, your intellectual powers, your immortal interests, perhaps, depend on the choice of this moment.—There is the door, and the key is in my hand.—Choose—choose!"—"And how comes the key in your hand? and what is the condition of my liberation?" said Stanton.

.. . . .

The explanation occupied several pages, which, to the torture of young Melmoth, were wholly illegible. It seemed, however, to have been rejected by Stanton with the utmost rage and horror, for Melmoth at last made out,—"Begone, monster, demon!—begone to your native place. Even this mansion of horror trembles to contain you; its walls sweat, and its floors quiver, while you tread them."

.. . . .

The conclusion of this extraordinary manuscript

was in such a state, that, in fifteen moldy and crumbling pages, Melmoth could hardly make out that number of lines. No antiquarian, unfolding with trembling hand the calcined leaves of an Herculaneum manuscript, and hoping to discover some lost lines of the Aeneis in Virgil's own autograph, or at least some unutterable abomination of Petronius or Martial, happily elucidatory of the mysteries of the Spintriae, or the orgies of the Phallic worshipers, ever pored with more luckless diligence, or shook a head of more hopeless despondency over his task. He could but just make out what tended rather to excite than assuage that feverish thirst of curiosity which was consuming his inmost soul. The manuscript told no more of Melmoth, but mentioned that Stanton was finally liberated from his confinement,—that his pursuit of Melmoth was incessant and indefatigable,—that he himself allowed it to be a species of insanity,—that while he acknowledged it to be the master passion, he also felt it the master torment of his life. He again visited the Continent, returned to England,— pursued, inquired, traced, bribed, but in vain. The being whom he had met thrice, under circumstances so extraordinary, he was fated never to encounter again IN HIS LIFETIME. At length, discovering that he had been born in Ireland, he resolved to go there,—went, and found his pursuit again fruitless, and his inquiries unanswered. The family knew nothing of him, or at least what they knew or imagined, they prudently refused to disclose to a stranger, and Stanton departed unsatisfied. It is remarkable, that he too, as appeared from many half-obliterated pages of the manuscript, never disclosed to mortal the particulars of their conversation in the madhouse; and the slightest allusion to it threw him into fits of rage and gloom equally singular and alarming. He left the manuscript, however, in the hands of the family, possibly deeming, from their incuriosity, their apparent indifference to their relative, or their obvious unacquaintance with reading of any kind, manuscript or books, his deposit would be safe. He seems, in fact, to have acted like men, who, in distress at sea, intrust their letters and dispatches to a bottle sealed, and commit it to the waves. The last lines of the manuscript that were legible, were sufficiently extraordinary…

. . . . .

"I have sought him everywhere.—The desire of meeting him once more is become as a burning fire within me,—it is the necessary condition of my existence. I have vainly sought him at last in Ireland, of which I find he is a native.—Perhaps our final meeting will be in… .

. . . . .

Such was the conclusion of the manuscript which

Melmoth found in his uncle's closet. When he had finished it, he sunk down on the table near which he had been reading it, his face hid in his folded arms, his senses reeling, his mind in a mingled state of stupor and excitement. After a few moments, he raised himself with an involuntary start, and saw the picture gazing at him from its canvas. He was within ten inches of it as he sat, and the proximity appeared increased by the strong light that was accidentally thrown on it, and its being the only representation of a human figure in the room. Melmoth felt for a moment as if he were about to receive an explanation from its lips.

He gazed on it in return,—all was silent in the house,—they were alone together. The illusion subsided at length: and as the mind rapidly passes to opposite extremes, he remembered the injunction of his uncle to destroy the portrait. He seized it;— his hand shook at first, but the moldering canvas appeared to assist him in the effort. He tore it from the frame with a cry half terrific, half triumphant,— it fell at his feet, and he shuddered as it fell. He expected to hear some fearful sounds, some unimaginable breathings of prophetic horror, follow this act of sacrilege, for such he felt it, to tear the portrait of his ancestor from his native walls. He paused and listened:—"There was no voice, nor any that answered;"—but as the wrinkled and torn canvas fell to the floor, its undulations gave the portrait the appearance of smiling. Melmoth felt horror indescribable at this transient and imaginary resuscitation of the figure. He caught it up, rushed into the next room, tore, cut, and hacked it in every direction, and eagerly watched the fragments that burned like tinder in the turf fire which had been lit in his room. As Melmoth saw the last blaze, he threw himself into bed, in hope of a deep and intense sleep. He had done what was required of him, and felt exhausted both in mind and body; but his slumber was not so sound as he had hoped for. The sullen light of the turf fire, burning but never blazing, disturbed him every moment. He turned and turned, but still there was the same red light glaring on, but not illuminating, the dusky furniture of the apartment. The wind was high that night, and as the creaking door swung on its hinges, every noise seemed like the sound of a hand struggling with the lock, or of a foot pausing on the threshold. But (for Melmoth never could decide) was it in a dream or not, that he saw the figure of his ancestor appear at the door?—hesitatingly as he saw him at first on the night of his uncle's death,—saw him enter the room, approach his bed, and heard him whisper, "You have burned me, then; but those are flames I can survive.—I am alive,—I am beside you." Melmoth started, sprung from his bed,—it was broad daylight. He looked round,—there was no human being in the room but himself. He felt a slight pain in the wrist of his right arm. He looked at it, it was black and blue, as from the recent gripe of a strong hand.